THIS WALKER BOOK BELONGS TO:

For Sallie
Derek

For Joanna & Lucy
John

First published 1985 by
Walker Books Ltd
87 Vauxhall Walk, London SE11 5HJ
as *Polar Bear Leaps*

This edition published 1988

Text © 1985, 1988 Derek Hall
Illustrations © 1985 John Butler

Printed in Italy by
Lito Roberto Terrazzi, Firenze

British Library Cataloguing in Publication Data
Hall, Derek, *1947-*
Laska the polar bear.
I. Title   II. Butler, John, *1952-*
III. Series
823'.914[J]
ISBN 0-7445-1111-9

Laska the Polar Bear

By Derek Hall

Illustrations by John Butler

WALKER BOOKS
LONDON

Laska the polar bear is big
enough to leave the den where he
was born. For the first time he
plays outside in the soft snow.

Soon it is time to go to the sea for food. Laska's mother is hungry. He rides high on her back, gripping her fur with excitement.

While his mother is busy
eating, Laska wanders off.
He stands up on his hind legs,
as tall as he can, to look out
over the Arctic sea.

Suddenly the ice breaks!
A small ice-floe carries Laska
away from the land, and
he is too young to swim!
He whimpers for his mother.

She roars to her cub in alarm.
Bravely he leaps across the gap
towards her. It is almost too far!
His paws slither on the icy shore.

Just in time his mother grasps him by the neck. She hauls him, dripping wet, from the water. Laska hangs limp and miserable from her strong jaws.

On firm land again, he shakes himself like a dog to dry his fur. His mother wants to find a safe place to sleep. Laska follows her like a shadow.

Now Laska is hungry.
His mother feeds him with her
milk. Then he snuggles up to
her warm body and goes to sleep.

MORE WALKER PAPERBACKS

BABIES' FIRST BOOKS

Jan Ormerod
Dad and Me
READING   SLEEPING
DAD'S BACK   MESSY BABY

PICTURE BOOKS
For The Very Young

Helen Oxenbury
Pippo
No. 1 TOM & PIPPO READ A STORY
No. 2 TOM & PIPPO MAKE A MESS
No. 3 TOM & PIPPO GO FOR A WALK
No. 4 TOM & PIPPO AND THE
　　　WASHING MACHINE
No. 5 TOM & PIPPO GO SHOPPING
No. 6 TOM & PIPPO'S DAY
No. 7 TOM & PIPPO IN THE GARDEN
No. 8 TOM & PIPPO SEE THE MOON

LEARNING FOR FUN
The Pre-School Years

Shirley Hughes
Nursery Collection
NOISY
COLOURS
BATHWATER'S HOT
ALL SHAPES AND SIZES
TWO SHOES, NEW SHOES
WHEN WE WENT TO THE PARK

John Burningham
Concept Books
COLOURS   ALPHABET
OPPOSITES   NUMBERS

Philippe Dupasquier
Busy Places
THE GARAGE   THE AIRPORT
THE BUILDING SITE
THE FACTORY   THE HARBOUR
THE RAILWAY STATION

Tony Wells   Puzzle Books
PUZZLE DOUBLES
ALLSORTS